Bodyparts

D1630611

Quiz No 204268
Bodyparts

Breslin, Theresa
B.L.: 3.9
Points: 1.0   MY

02907

Bodyparts

Theresa Breslin
Illustrated by Janek Matysiak

A & C Black · London

GRAFFIX

First paperback edition 1998
Reprinted 1999

First published 1998 in hardback by
A & C Black (Publishers) Ltd
35 Bedford Row, London WC1R 4JH

ISBN 0-7136-4904-6

A CIP catalogue record for this book is available from
the British Library.

Printed in Great Britain by William Clowes Ltd,
Beccles, Suffolk.

Chapter One

Blast!

Shaun stopped half-way down the stairs from the Genetic Clone Unit. He'd just looked at his wrist to check the time and realised his watch was missing.

Blast. Must have left my watch in one of the lockers...

5

He walked quickly among the experiment benches. Microscopes and ray tubes cast giant shadows and grotesque shapes on the walls and roof. He hurried past the Mutant Human Parts Section where the deformed organs were kept sealed in air-controlled tanks.

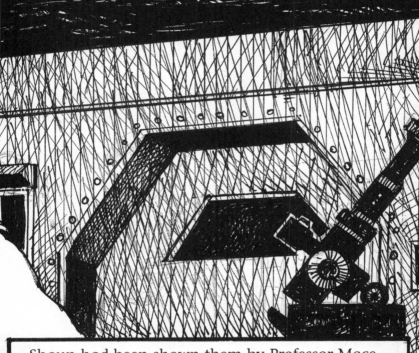

Shaun had been shown them by Professor Mace when he first joined the research team. These life forms were kept alive in case they were needed for future research. Shaun had been told they were completely secure, but he always felt uneasy when he was near them. What weird things they had created in the late 1990s before scientists had cracked the secret of proper genetic cloning!

The Genetic Clone Unit where replacement human organs were grown had to be very hygienic. This was the third time in the last week that something like this had happened. Equipment getting broken, things left in a mess.

The government inspection was due any day, and they couldn't afford to get sloppy. More funding was needed to carry on with their new project, the Advanced Growth Culture. If the Culture worked then it would be possible to grow spare human bodyparts in days rather than months. Shaun believed they were far ahead of any other research lab. With the extra money they could complete their research.

Shaun moved on. Behind him, on the wall, a shadow moved too.

The Locker Room was at the far end of the lab. As Shaun opened the door he automatically raised his hand to flick on the light switch, but then he stopped. The light in the Locker Room was already on.

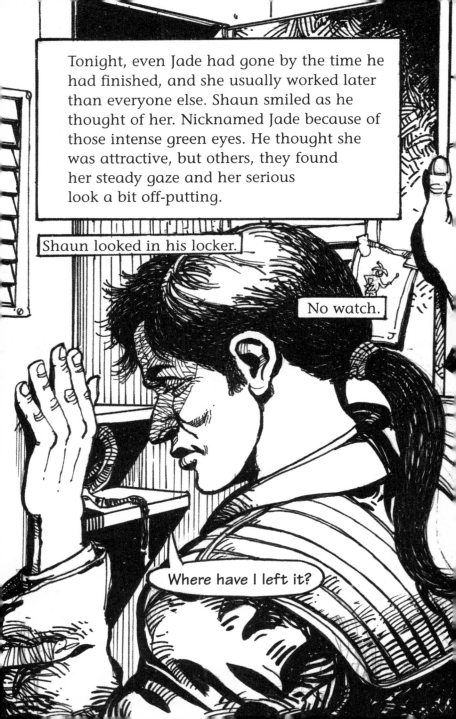

The lab rules were very strict. Everything had to be dirt-free. Not even deodorants or after-shaves were allowed. Shaun crouched down on the floor, glanced around him, and sniffed again. The smell seemed to be coming from one of the air vents at floor level.

Then he noticed a few faint wisps of smoke. Something was burning!

Better get out of here!

14

His eyes searched desperately until he found the fire alarm. Quickly he broke the glass and pressed the button. Nothing happened.

C'mon, c'mon!

Shaun stared at it for a second or two. His hands were beginning to sweat. What could he do now?

He knelt down and looked at the vent. He would never be able to prise it open. It was screwed tightly to the wall, and now the smoke was pouring through it rapidly.

23

24

Shaun thought for a moment. Then he got up
and examined the catch on the Locker Room door.
It seemed okay.

Shaun picked up the screwdriver and knelt down beside the vent. In a few moments he had unscrewed the cover. It fell with a clatter on the floor. He stuck his hand inside and felt about in the wall cavity.

Got it!

He pulled out his hand, and with it a bundle of charred rags.

These have been soaked in petrol.

I was right. The fire wasn't an accident. Someone is trying to sabotage our research.

Chapter Three

'Sabotage?' said Professor Mace the next morning when Shaun told him of last night's events.

Sabotage.

Shaun laid the remains of the burnt cloths in front of the Professor.

This was not an accident. I asked Gabriel to take a look at the alarm, and he confirmed that it had been tampered with.

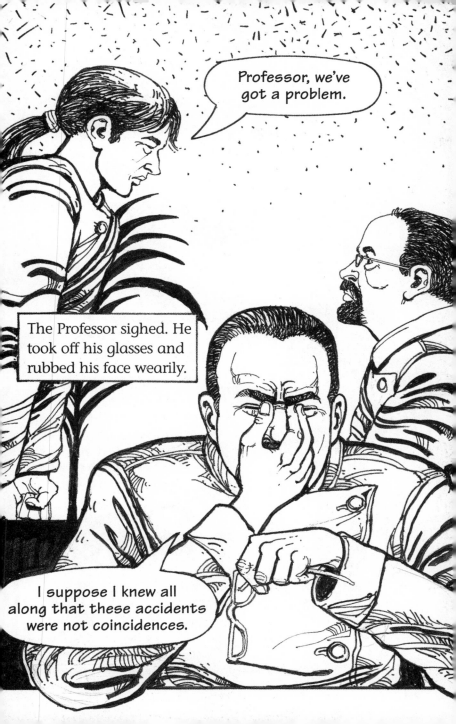

The Professor polished his glasses
carefully and put them back on.

Jade, thought Shaun. Was it just by chance that she turned up last night when she did? Or had she been hiding in the lab all along and then changed her mind about letting him die when she heard him calling out?

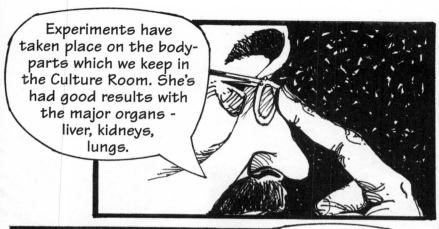

Experiments have taken place on the body-parts which we keep in the Culture Room. She's had good results with the major organs - liver, kidneys, lungs.

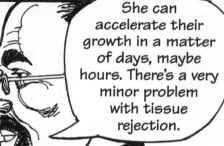

She can accelerate their growth in a matter of days, maybe hours. There's a very minor problem with tissue rejection.

Apart from that we are almost ready for live human trials.

Isn't that a bit risky? You'd need a terminal patient. Who else would volunteer?

'I have,' said a voice from the doorway.

Chapter Four

Shaun turned. Rees stood there. His voice was shaking with excitement, and he ran his fingers nervously through his hair.

Jade is setting up a trial for later this week.

Wow! She must be pretty sure that it will work.

'Well, I'm not so sure,' the Professor spoke abruptly. 'I'll see Jade and speak to you both later.'

He stood up and strode from the room.

38

Three days later Jade was in the Culture Room, ready to proceed. The Professor called his team to the Changing Room where they would put on the huge white "bunny-suit" overalls and helmets. Then they would have a clean air shower before going through the air lock into the Culture Room where the bodyparts were grown.

Shaun and Rees climbed into their bunny-suits and sat waiting for Kelly.

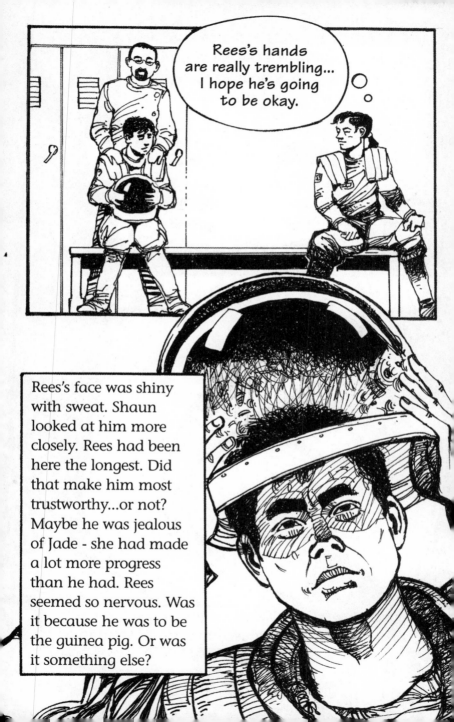

The Professor must have noticed it too. Shaun saw him speaking quietly to Rees. He placed his hand on the young man's shoulder.

Rees shook his head. 'Okay then,' said the Professor. 'You two go on. I'll chase up Kelly. I want her to take notes during the test.'

Chapter Five

They were in the Culture Room and both Jade and Rees had placed their arms through holes in a large glass incubator. Rees had removed one glove. Jade had replaced her gloves with surgical ones.

Still want to go through with it?

Yes.

I'll **do** a quick pre-trial test while we're waiting for Kelly and the Professor.

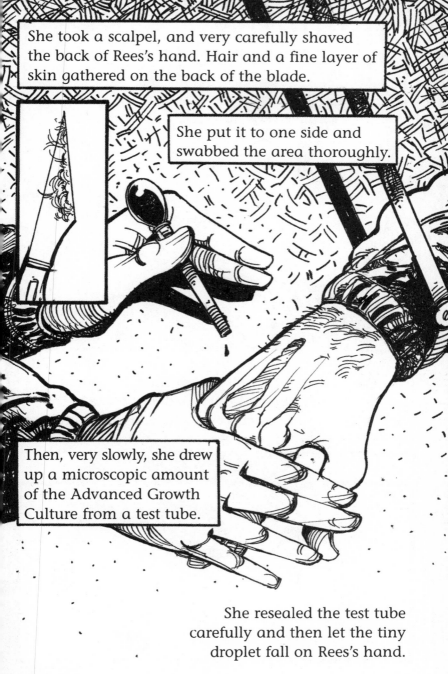

She took a scalpel, and very carefully shaved the back of Rees's hand. Hair and a fine layer of skin gathered on the back of the blade.

She put it to one side and swabbed the area thoroughly.

Then, very slowly, she drew up a microscopic amount of the Advanced Growth Culture from a test tube.

She resealed the test tube carefully and then let the tiny droplet fall on Rees's hand.

Behind him Shaun heard the hiss of the air lock and he glanced round. He read Kelly's name badge on the overall of the figure at the door, and gave her a wave. Then he turned back to look again into the incubator.

My God!

47

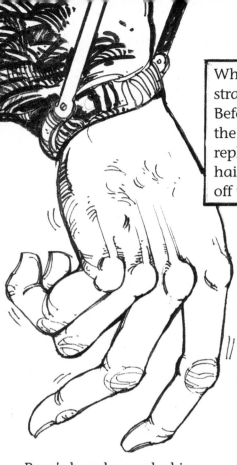

What Shaun saw was straight from a sci-fi movie. Before his eyes the skin on the back of Rees's hand was replacing itself. The very hairs which had been cut off were regrowing.

I don't believe it!

Rees's hand was shaking uncontrollably.

I'll get the Professor. He must see this!

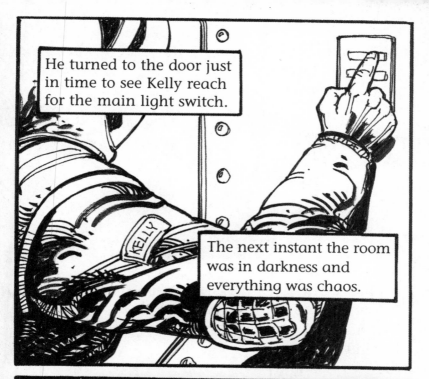

He turned to the door just in time to see Kelly reach for the main light switch.

The next instant the room was in darkness and everything was chaos.

Jade screamed and Rees called out, but their cries were deafened by the sound of shattering glass.

As Shaun moved to help them he was pushed roughly to the floor. Then he heard the air lock hiss once more.

Suddenly Jade grabbed Shaun's arm.

Look! The Culture!

She pointed inside the wrecked incubator to where the test tube had rested on its stand. It was now empty.

The Advanced Growth Culture. It's gone!

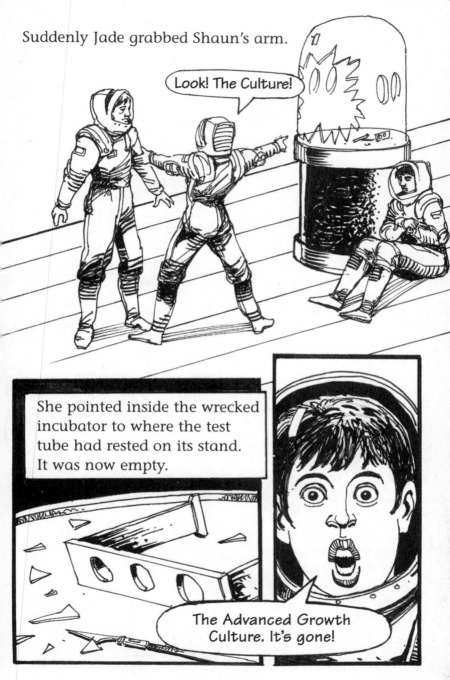

Chapter Six

Jade was almost hysterical. She grabbed the front of Shaun's suit and began to shake him.

He strode over to the door and hit the panic button.

Now let's see if Rees is okay and then we'll go back to the Changing Room and find the Professor.

Right...that will make sure no-one leaves the building. Gabriel will be here in seconds.

Shaun watched as Jade wound a protective cover over Rees's hand. It was scary. Apart from one or two small patches the Culture hadn't reached, his hand had completely healed over. The skin had a healthy firm appearance.

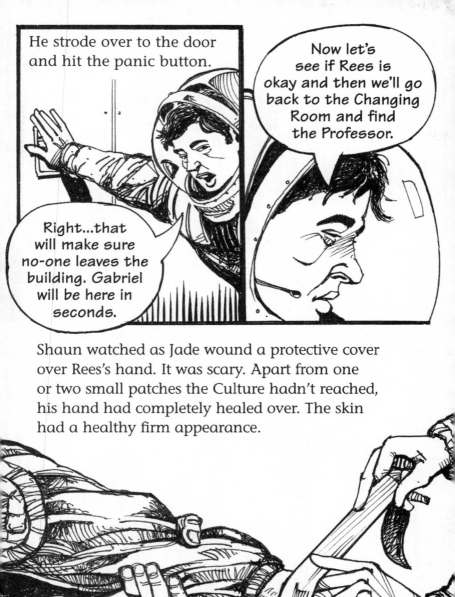

The Professor was right. This was worth millions.

The three of them quickly returned through the air lock. As they opened the Changing Room door they saw Kelly sitting with her bunny-suit on and her helmet in her hand.

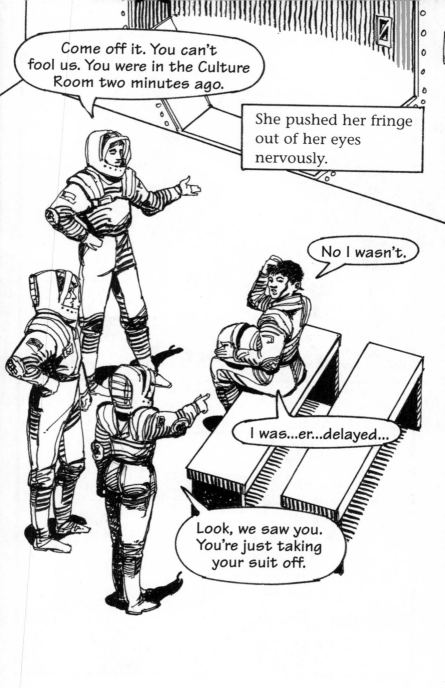

55

Shaun breathed a sigh of relief and told Gabriel exactly what had happened. Kelly gasped when she heard Shaun say that he'd just seen her enter the Culture Room, switch off the lights and take the Culture.

Kelly blushed, and glanced at Gabriel.

Chapter Seven

'I saw him a moment ago,' said Gabriel. 'As I came through the lab, he was hurrying into the Mutant Human Parts Section.'

Why would he go there, when there's an alarm on?

He's been spending a lot of time in there recently. Some of those... mistakes...date back to his early days in this Unit.

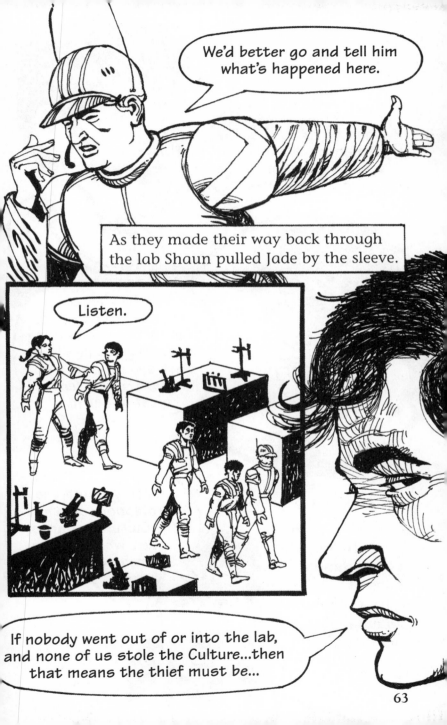

63

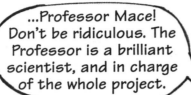

...Professor Mace! Don't be ridiculous. The Professor is a brilliant scientist, and in charge of the whole project.

Yes, but he told me earlier this week that he knew something was wrong yet he didn't alert security. He also asked me to keep quiet about it...

'He started this whole Unit,' said Jade. 'He wouldn't do anything to harm it.'

'Just a minute,' Shaun pulled her to a halt.

Both you and the Professor said that the Culture is dangerous... what did you mean exactly?

You saw what it did in seconds, using only a tiny droplet. Imagine more of it, and it not being used to heal. You could grow mutant species and enlarge them to create monsters...

Jade's voice tailed off. Her eyes met Shaun's.

My God!

They both began to run.

The Professor turned, and they could see that he had the test tube containing the Culture in his hand.

The Professor laughed, a high-pitched giggle, and removed the stopper from the test tube.

Suddenly Gabriel leapt from behind and grabbed the Professor's arm. For an instant he had him held fast but the Professor struggled and the test tube slipped from his grasp and began to fall...

Shaun dived for his life.

Before long a medical team arrived. Kelly and Gabriel helped the Professor to his feet. He turned as he left the lab.

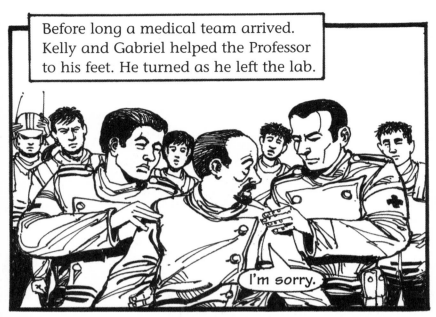

Then they all left the lab together. Gabriel followed Shaun and Jade outside and locked the lab door securely.

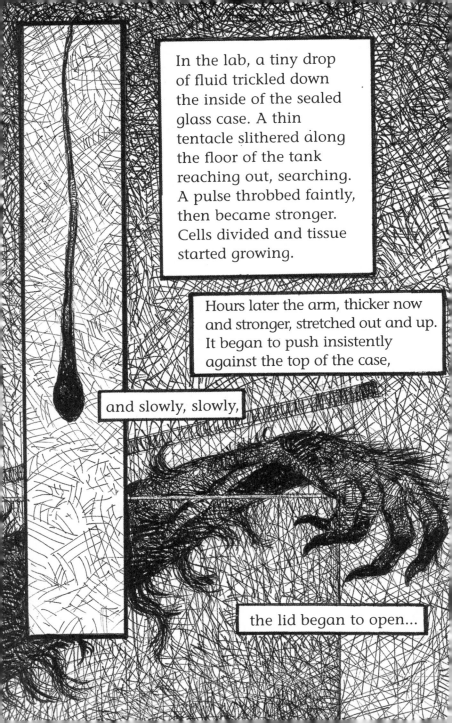

In the lab, a tiny drop of fluid trickled down the inside of the sealed glass case. A thin tentacle slithered along the floor of the tank reaching out, searching. A pulse throbbed faintly, then became stronger. Cells divided and tissue started growing.

Hours later the arm, thicker now and stronger, stretched out and up. It began to push insistently against the top of the case,

and slowly, slowly,

the lid began to open...